Boogers
and Snot

Boogers and Snot

A Grandfather's Story

Larry Gatlin with Parker

Photos by Ishy (Janis) Gatlin

EAKIN PRESS ⟨EP⟩ Austin, Texas

FIRST EDITION
Copyright © 2003
By Larry Gatlin
Published in the United States of America
By Eakin Press
A Division of Sunbelt Media, Inc.
P.O. Drawer 90159 Austin, Texas 78709-0159
email: sales@eakinpress.com
🖳 website: www.eakinpress.com 🖳
1 2 3 4 5 6 7 8 9
1-57168-820-X PB
1-57168-821-8 HB
Library of Congress Control Number: 2003115381

To my papa,
Clib Doan,
who taught me
what bein' a great
papa is all about.
I hope I'm half as good a papa
as he was.

—"Papa" Gatlin

It was Christmastime. People all over the world were celebrating the birth of the Christ Child and taking time to be thankful for their many blessings. In Texas, a grandfather was so thankful and happy that he decided to write a Christmas song as a special gift for his three-year-old granddaughter, Parker.

As Papa held his rosy pink granddaughter, some of the words for the song started coming into his head, and he began to sing. But in the middle of his joyful new song, Papa stopped because Parker started wheezing and sneezing and coughing. You see, she had a very bad cold.

apa felt really awful that he couldn't do anything to make her feel better, so he said a little prayer.

Parker seemed to get better for a moment, but after a while she started to cry. Papa thought he would try his song again. But the Christmas song had taken a new direction:

"Well, boogers and snot is what I got.
I got 'em in my pretty little nose."

Parker stopped crying and looked up at her Papa. He sang some more:

"I'm a little toot, but I sure am cute. . ."

Papa held the high note a long time, and Parker started to giggle.

"And that's just the way it goes."

The little girl's face broke into a big smile and she said, "Papa, that is a silly song, but I like it because you made it up just for me." So, he took his guitar and began playing and singing louder and more joyfully than before.

"Well, boogers and snot is what I got.
I got 'em in my pretty little nose.
I'm a little toot, but I sure am cute. . .
And that's just the way it goes."

That night Papa sang a solo at the church Christmas celebration. He gathered all the little children together in front of their mothers and fathers and grandmothers and grandfathers to teach them the new song. He said:

"I would like to thank God for the precious gift of the Christ Child, and I would like to offer a gift back to God and to the Christ Child in the name of another precious gift, my granddaughter, Parker, who is at home sick with a bad cold. Here's how it goes:

"Well, boogers and snot is what I got. . ."

The children started laughing, so he stopped.

"Now, just a minute," he said. "We're all God's children, and we've all had a bad cold before in our lives. This song is going to make us feel better the next time we have a cold. So here we go. . .

"Well, boogers and snot. . ."

After he had finished the first verse, he stopped again and said, "Now, I know that doesn't sound like a Christmas song, but wait 'til you hear the rest of it.

"Well, down came love from heaven above
'Neath the Bethlehem Star
Teach the little children only love
'Cause love is what they are."

He asked the audience to sing the chorus.

"All together now!

Boogers and snot . . ."

The grownups joined in because they knew in their hearts that we are, in fact, all God's kids. And He's made us in almost every color of the rainbow. Some are big kids, some are little kids. Some are short, and some are tall. Some are young kids, and some are old. But all kids are the same in God's eyes. And they knew that at one time or another, *all* God's kids have had:

"Boogers and snot. . ."

Everyone went home that night with a new understanding of what it is like to be a kid. And everyone felt more grateful for the Christ Child.

Papa tiptoed into Parker's room later that night while she was sleeping. She was breathing easier now, and he sang very quietly to her:

"Well, down came love from heaven above
'Neath the Bethlehem Star
Teach the little children only love
'Cause love is what they are."

He kissed her on the nose and said, "Love is what you are, Parker, and you are loved."

It was a warm December night in Texas, so on his way home Papa put the top down on his little car and sang at the top of his lungs to the moon and the stars and the heavens and to God on High:

"Well, boogers and snot is what I got. . ."

Thank goodness he was a mile away or he would have awakened his little granddaughter, whose bad cold was much, much better now. Thank God!

BOOGERS AND SNOT

Well, boogers and snot is what I've got. I got 'em in my pretty little nose. I'm a little toot, but I sure am cute. And that's just the way it goes. Down came love from heaven a-bove 'neath the Bethlehem star. Teach the little chil-dren o-nly love, 'cause that's just what they are. Well,

ISHY PARKER PAPA

About the Author

Larry Gatlin started in the music business in 1954, when he and his brothers sang for ten cents a week on a morning radio show in Abilene, Texas. Larry was only six years old at the time. Since that debut, he has flourished as a singer, songwriter, author, and actor and overcome personal struggles to become a devoted husband, father, grandfather, and re-dedicated Christian.

While attending the University of Houston on a football scholarship, majoring in English and eventually law, he couldn't resist being drawn to Music Row in Nashville, Tennessee. His brothers joined him, and the Gatlin Brothers were soon recording an impressive string of number-one records, with hits like "Broken Lady," "Houston (Means I'm One Day Closer to You)," and "All the Gold in California." Larry's international fame has grown with film appearances, a stint on Broadway (*Will Rogers Follies*), a critically acclaimed autobiography (*All the Gold in California*), and a Carnegie Hall appearance with Skitch Henderson and the New York Pops.

Now living in Austin, Texas, he regularly performs in Branson, Missouri, and maintains a busy personal and professional schedule. But the most important things in his life are his faith, his family, and his friends—especially his "Doodlebug," Parker.